WILLIAM
& THE MISSING
MASTERPIECE

For Kate, for all the help and cake along the way – H.

For Mia Wallace, with thanks and love to Isobel, Maddie and, of course, Kate – W.

A TEMPLAR BOOK

First published in hardback and softback in the UK in 2014 by Templar Publishing,
an imprint of The Templar Company Limited,
Deepdene Lodge, Deepdene Avenue, Dorking, Surrey, RH5 4AT, UK
www.templarco.co.uk

First edition

ISBN 978-1-84877-427-8 (hardback)
ISBN 978-1-78370-078-3 (softback)

Edited by Jenny Broom
Designed by Mike Jolley

Printed in China

HELEN HANCOCKS

WILLIAM
& THE MISSING
MASTERPIECE

templar publishing

William, the international cat of mystery, was planning a holiday when he was interrupted by a telephone call.

On the line was Monsieur Gruyère, from a gallery in Paris.

"A terrible thing has happened!" he shouted. "Our most famous painting, the Mona Cheesa, has been stolen!"

STOLEN!

"The timing couldn't be worse! It's National Cheese Week in
Paris and my gallery had planned to hold an exhibition in its honour…
William, can you help us find the missing masterpiece?"

William agreed at once to help and began packing his bags.
His holiday would have to wait.

Soon William was in Paris,
the city of art and cheese.

HOMAGE TO FROMAGE GALA

CHEESE FESTIVAL

He headed to the gallery to get to work on the case.

HOMAGE TO FROMAGE
GALA

CHEESE FESTIVAL

William arrived at
the scene of the crime.
Monsieur Gruyère showed him
the museum's fine paintings, and the
gap where the Mona Cheesa used to hang.

"No suspects were seen," he said,
"and no evidence has been found!
I fear we have lost the Mona Cheesa forever!"
It seemed that William had his work cut out.

William examined the room. At first, there didn't seem to be much evidence.

On closer inspection, however, William found…

a small hole in the skirting board…

and a strand of red wool.

This was all very perplexing.
William decided to call in on two
of his artist-friends, Fifi Le Brie
and Henri Roquefort, to see if they
had any bright ideas.

Alas, Fifi and Henri couldn't help.

"We have been busy preparing for a painting competition, which opens tonight at the gallery," said Henri.

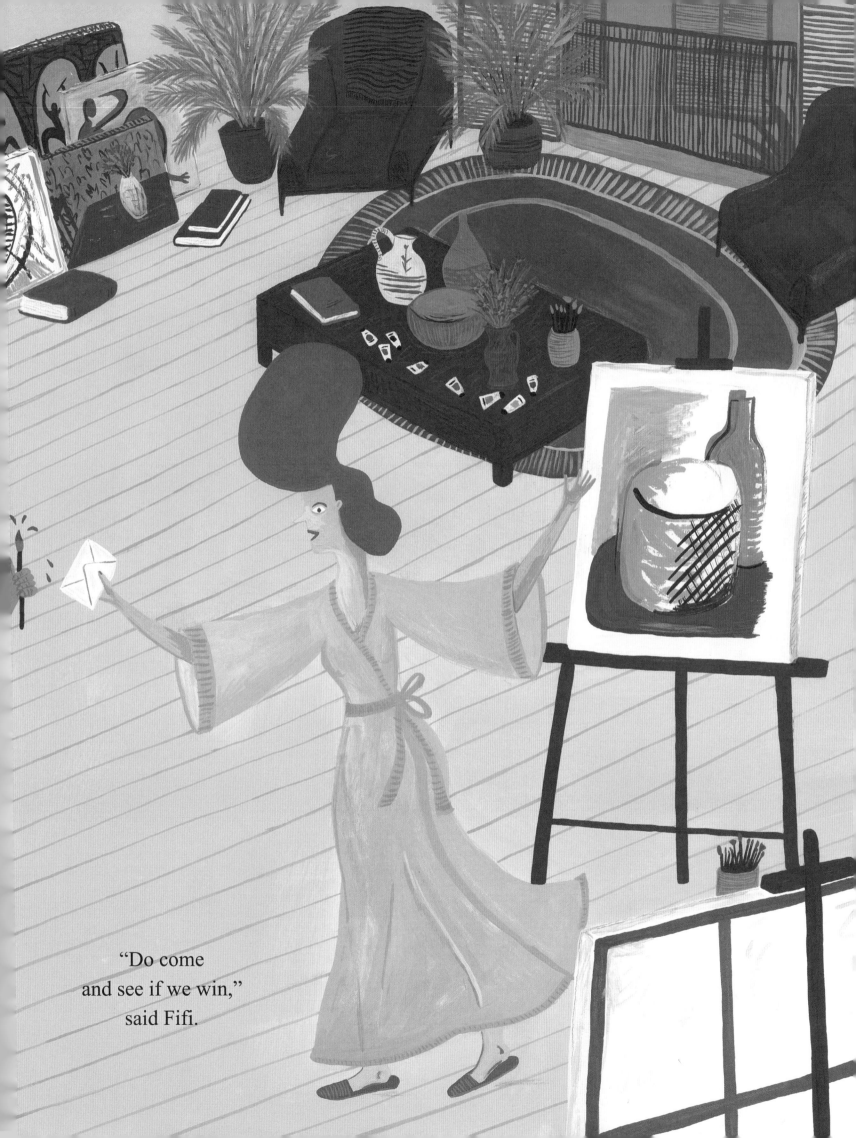

"Do come
and see if we win,"
said Fifi.

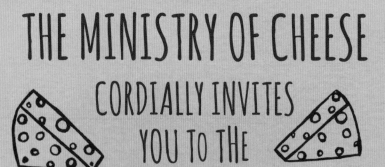

THE MINISTRY OF CHEESE

CORDIALLY INVITES
YOU TO tHE

HOMAGE tO FROMAGE

ANNUAL ART GALA

A TROPHY AND A YEAR'S SUPPLY OF CHEESE FOR THE WINNER!

William decided to go. Perhaps somebody at the event
would have some information about the missing masterpiece.
Meanwhile, he had all afternoon to ponder the case…

But first it was time for a spot of lunch. He set off for his favourite cafe.

William was just taking a digestive pause from his meal
when an unusual character caught his eye.

The shady figure was wearing a hat and bright red woollen scarf
(which seemed strange on such a sunny day), and was carrying
a large package.

William decided to see what he was up to.

William used one of his best disguises to make sure
he stayed hidden whilst he kept an eye on things.

He watched the shady figure enter a fancy dress shop,
and leave with another mysterious parcel.

He sneakily followed the shady figure down the street,

through the park,

and over the bridge.

But before William could find out where he was going…

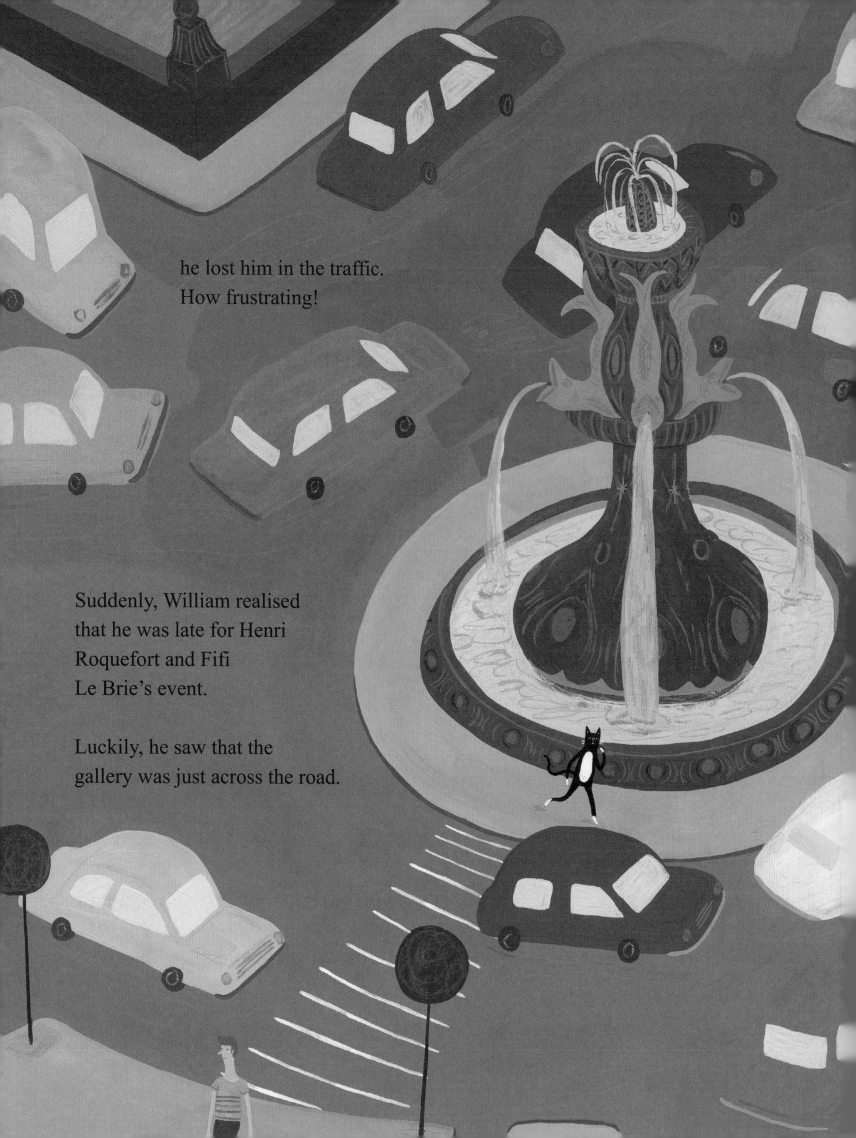

he lost him in the traffic.
How frustrating!

Suddenly, William realised
that he was late for Henri
Roquefort and Fifi
Le Brie's event.

Luckily, he saw that the
gallery was just across the road.

He headed straight inside.
He would continue his investigations tomorrow.

Inside, William met Monsieur Gruyère, who was judging the competition, and his friends, Henri and Fifi.

They showed William their paintings, and explained that quite a stir had been made by a surprise last-minute entry.

"It is a wonderful painting!" said Monsieur Gruyère.
"But nobody has heard of this artist before."

William stared hard at the new painting.
Something about it seemed very familiar…

William thought back over his day and began to piece together the clues.

There had been the wool…

the hole in the skirting board…

the shady figure carrying a large package…

the fancy dress shop…

the mysterious painting…

and the prize, a year's supply of—

"CHEESE!"

William exclaimed, and he dashed off to find Monsieur Gruyère.

Monsieur Gruyère was just about to announce that the mystery painter had won the competition, when William burst in.

"Wait!" he shouted. "This artist is a fraud!" And with that he peeled off the painting's cunning disguise to reveal…

the Mona Cheesa!

The crowd gasped in surprise.

"Stop that man!" William ordered, as he suddenly spotted the shady figure in the audience trying to make a getaway.

William tugged at the shady figure's red woollen scarf and the mystery of the missing masterpiece finally unravelled.

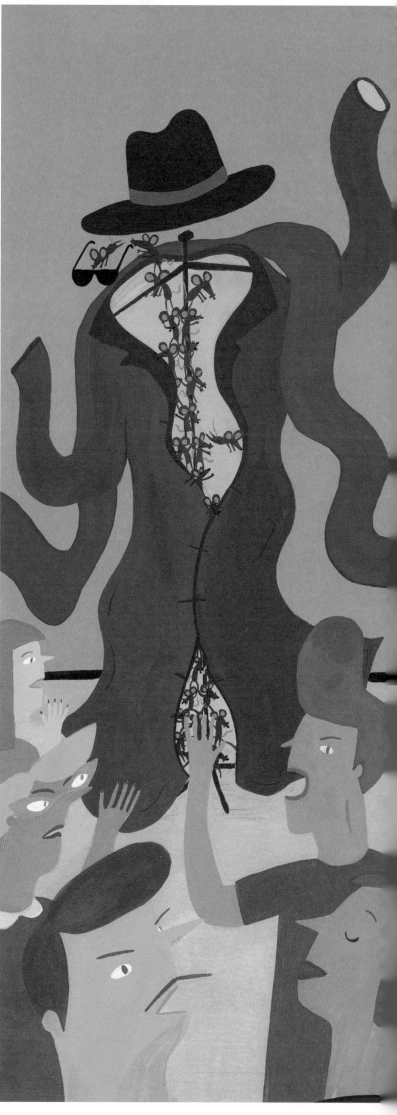

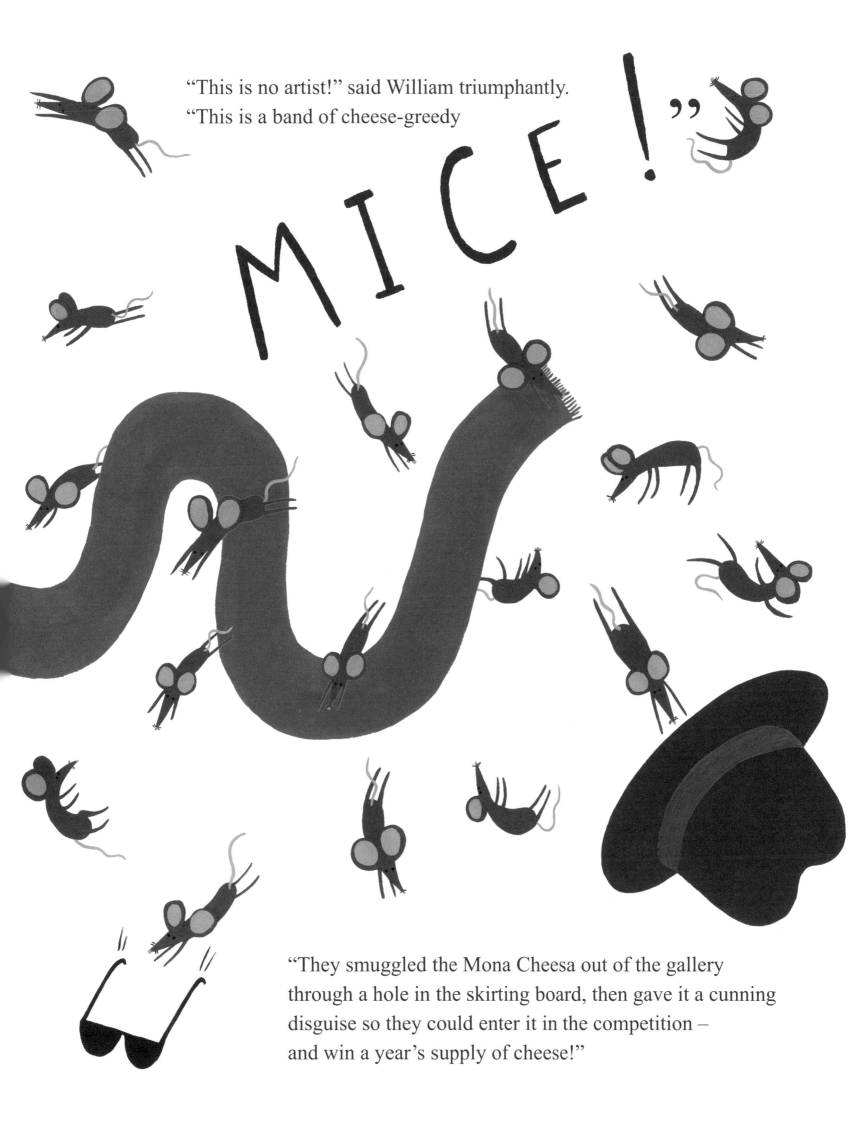

"This is no artist!" said William triumphantly.
"This is a band of cheese-greedy

MICE!"

"They smuggled the Mona Cheesa out of the gallery
through a hole in the skirting board, then gave it a cunning
disguise so they could enter it in the competition –
and win a year's supply of cheese!"

Everybody was delighted with William's discovery.
Monsieur Gruyère had the Mona Cheesa back.

Fifi Le Brie and Henri Roquefort won
joint first prize at the Homage to Fromage.

William could finally take his holiday.

And as for the mice…

POLICE ON HUNT TO TRAP PICTURE-PINCHING MICE

"No Roquefort will be left unturned!" vowed police as a nation-wide search to catch the band of villainous mice got underway.

The robbers had thought their mission to steal the Mona Cheesa a 'feta-compli' as they were handed first prize at the annual Homage to Fromage competition. However, in a dramatic turn of events, their cunning disguise was unmasked by international cat of mystery, William. The furry rogues then fled the scene of the crime.

"To see the thieves go unpunished really grates,"

said Monsieur Gruyère, custodian of the Mona Cheesa.

Police urged the public to stay alert, saying the suspects, described as "small and mousy", had gone underground but were likely to strike again. "Do not underestimate these villains," warned police, "they will do almost anything to get their next cheese fix and could be hiding in a skirting board near you."

FIN.